D1001507

Valentine's Day

A Level Two Reader

By Cynthia Klingel and Robert B. Noyed

The Child's World®

I love you! It is time for

Valentine's Day.

Valentine's Day takes place on February 14. It is a day for showing love and friendship.

Valentine's Day started long ago in other countries. It was sometimes called by other names.

Now, people all over the world celebrate Valentine's Day. Red, pink, and white are valentine colors.

Many people send cards called valentines to their family and friends. Many valentines are in the shape of a heart.

Valentines say sweet and silly things. Many valentines have poems.

Many people give flowers on Valentine's Day. Red roses are a special valentine flower.

Candy is a special valentine treat. Stores sell heart-shaped boxes full of candy.

Many people give flowers on Valentine's Day. Red roses are a special valentine flower.

Candy is a special valentine treat. Stores sell heart-shaped boxes full of candy.

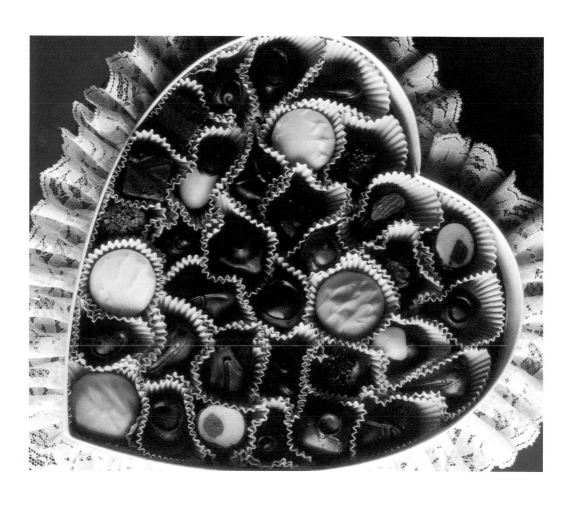

Valentine's Day is a day for love. Some people get married on Valentine's Day.

Think of someone you love and say, "Happy Valentine's Day! Will you be my valentine?"

Index

candy, 16

cards, 11

colors, 8

family, 11

flowers, 15

friendship, 4, 11

heart, 11, 16

love, 3, 4, 19, 20

poems, 12

valentines, 12

To Find Out More

Books

Bulla, Clyde Robert. *The Story of Valentine's Day.* New York: HarperCollins Children's Books, 1999.

Ross, Kathy. *Crafts for Valentine's Day.* Brookfield, Conn.: Millbrook Press, 1995.

Wing, Natasha. *The Night Before Valentine's Day.* New York: Penguin Putnam Books for Young Readers, 2000.

Web Sites

Celebrate! Holidays in the U.S.A.: St. Valentine's Day
http://www.usis.usemb.se/Holidays/celebrate/valentins.html
For an article about Valentine's Day from a U.S. embassy.

Love Letters
http://www.usps.gov/letters/volume2/love-main.html
For famous love letters in history.

Note to Parents and Educators

Welcome to Wonder Books®! These books provide text at three different levels for beginning readers to practice and strengthen their reading skills. Additionally, the use of nonfiction text provides readers the valuable opportunity to *read to learn*, not just to learn to read.

These leveled readers allow children to choose books at their level of reading confidence and performance. Nonfiction Level One books offer beginning readers simple language, word choice, and sentence structure as well as a word list. Nonfiction Level Two books feature slightly more difficult vocabulary, longer sentences, and longer total text. In the back of each Nonfiction Level Two book are an index and a list of books and Web sites for finding out more information. Nonfiction Level Three books continue to extend word choice and length of text. In the back of each Nonfiction Level Three book are a glossary, an index, and a list of books and Web sites for further research.

State and national standards in reading and language arts emphasize using nonfiction at all levels of reading development. Wonder Books® fill the historical void in nonfiction material for primary grade readers with the additional benefit of a leveled text.

About the Authors

Cynthia Klingel has worked as a high school English teacher and an elementary school teacher. She is currently the curriculum director for a Minnesota school district. Cynthia lives with her family in Mankato, Minnesota.

Robert B. Noyed started his career as a newspaper reporter. Since then, he has worked in school communications and public relations at the state and national level. Robert lives with his family in Brooklyn Center, Minnesota.

Published by The Child's World®, Inc.
PO Box 326
Chanhassen, MN 55317-0326
800-599-READ
www.childsworld.com

Special thanks to the first grade students of Middleton School, their parents, and teacher (Julie Marcus) for their help and cooperation in preparing this book.

Photo Credits
© Photri, Inc.: cover
© Richard Hutchings/PhotoEdit: 17
© Romie Flanagan: 2, 5, 10, 21
© Stock Montage Inc.: 6, 13
© Tony Arruza/CORBIS: 18
© Tony Freeman/PhotoEdit: 9, 14

Project Coordination: Editorial Directions, Inc.
Photo Research: Alice K. Flanagan

Library of Congress Cataloging-in-Publication Data
Klingel, Cynthia Fitterer.
Valentine's Day / by Cynthia Klingel and Robert B. Noyed.
    p. cm. — (Wonder books)
Includes bibliographical references and index.
ISBN 1-56766-957-3 (lib. bdg. : alk. paper)
1. Valentine's Day—Juvenile literature. [1. Valentine's Day.]
I. Noyed, Robert B. II. Title. III. Wonder books (Chanhassen, Minn.)
GT4925 .K55 2001
394.2618—dc21
                                00-011364